THE FAMILY CAR SONGBOOK

On The Road AGAIN

20 Sing-Along Favorites to Make the Miles Fly By!

RUNNING PRESS
KIDS
PHILADELPHIA·LONDON

© 2005 by Running Press

Printed in China

9 8 7 6 5 4 3 2
Digit on the right indicates the number of this printing

Library of Congress Control Number: 2004118133

ISBN 0-7624-2210-6

Designed by Frances J. Soo Ping Chow
Illustrated by Jason Tharp
Edited by Elizabeth Encarnacion
Typography: Gill Sans, Lo Type, Memphis, and Rockwell

This book may be ordered by mail from the publisher.
Please include $2.50 for postage and handling.
But try your bookstore first!

Published by Running Press Kids, an imprint of
Running Press Book Publishers
125 South Twenty-second Street
Philadelphia, Pennsylvania 19103-4399

Visit us on the web!
www.runningpress.com

Playlist

Do Your Ears Hang Low?

Traditional

This traditional song sounds like nonsense, but it has its origins in the American Revolutionary War. British drummers kept their rope drums tied very tightly and may have sung this song to tease the drummers of the Continental Army about keeping their ropes too loose, allowing the "ears" of the drum to hang low. For extra fun, try singing the song faster and faster each time while performing the hand motions listed below!

Do your ears hang low? Do they wob - ble to and fro? Can you

tie them in a knot? Can you tie them in a bow? Can you

swing them o - ver your shoul-der like a Con - ti - nen-tal sol - dier? Do your

ears hang low?

HAND MOTIONS

EARS HANG LOW: hang your hands below your ears

WOBBLE TO AND FRO: move your hands from side to side
without moving your wrists

TIE THEM IN A KNOT: tie an invisible knot in the air

TIE THEM IN A BOW: tie an invisible bow in the air,
pulling the loops of the bow out dramatically

SWING THEM OVER YOUR SHOULDER: lift both hands over one shoulder

LIKE A CONTINENTAL SOLDIER: salute with your hand against your forehead

EARS HANG LOW: repeat first action

The Caisson Song
(The Caissons Go Rolling Along)

Lyrics by Edmund Gruber

Lieutenant Edmund Gruber wrote this classic military song about the spirit of the field artillery soldiers whose job was to keep the caissons, two-wheeled carts that carried ammunition, moving across difficult terrain. The tune was eventually paired with new words and adopted as the official song of the U.S. Army.

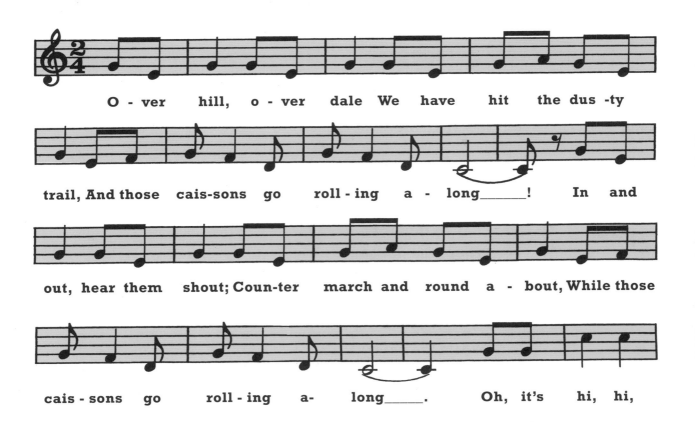

O - ver hill, o - ver dale We have hit the dus -ty trail, And those cais-sons go roll - ing a - long_____! In and out, hear them shout; Coun-ter march and round a - bout, While those cais - sons go roll - ing a- long_____. Oh, it's hi, hi,

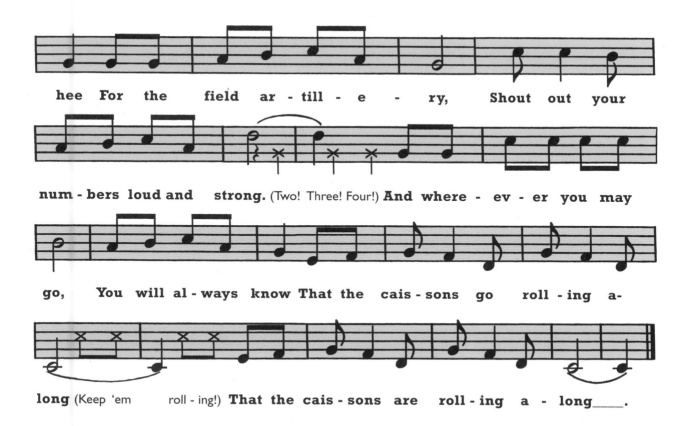

hee For the field ar - till - e - ry, Shout out your

num - bers loud and strong. (Two! Three! Four!) **And** where - ev - er you may

go, You will al - ways know That the cais - sons go roll - ing a-

long (Keep 'em roll - ing!) **That** the cais - sons are roll - ing a - long____.

2

At the front, day and night,
Where the doughboys dig and fight—
And those caissons go rolling along!—
Our barrage will be there,
Adding to the rockets' glare,
While the caissons go rolling along.

Chorus

3

Hear that whine? It's a shell!
Hit the dirt and dig like hell,
While the caissons go rolling along.
Comes the boom, stand up higher,
Take good aim, return the fire,
Help those caissons go rolling along!

Chorus

4

Through the mud, through the lines,
Past the trenches and the mines,
Where the caissons go rolling along,
We won't rest till we see
Our brave lads taste victory,
And the caissons stop rolling along.

Chorus

There's a Hole in the Bucket

Traditional German-American song

Going to be in the car for a while? This traditional German-American folk song has tons of verses to help the trip go by faster. To make it more interesting, pick one of the parts and sing back and forth with your brother or sister, getting totally into character.

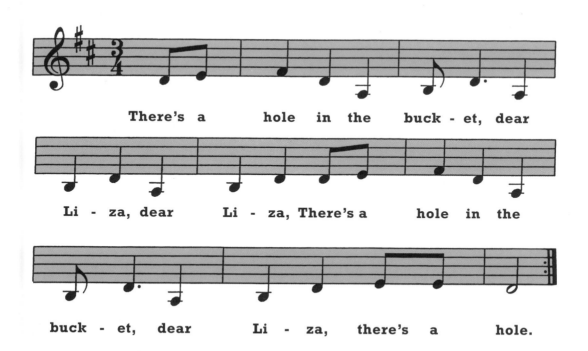

There's a hole in the buck - et, dear

Li - za, dear Li - za, There's a hole in the

buck - et, dear Li - za, there's a hole.

2

Well, fix it, dear Henry, dear Henry, dear Henry,
Well fix it, dear Henry, dear Henry, go fix it.

3

With what shall I fix it, dear Liza, dear Liza,
With what shall I fix it, dear Liza, with what?

4

With a straw, dear Henry, dear Henry, dear Henry,
With a straw, dear Henry, dear Henry, with a straw.

5

But the straw is too long, dear Liza, dear Liza,
But the straw is too long, dear Liza, too long.

6

Then cut it, dear Henry, dear Henry, dear Henry,
Then cut it, dear Henry, dear Henry, then cut it.

7

With what shall I cut it, dear Liza, dear Liza,
With what shall I cut it, dear Liza, with what?

8

With a knife, dear Henry, dear Henry, dear Henry,
With a knife, dear Henry, dear Henry, with a knife.

9

But the knife is too dull, dear Liza, dear Liza,
But the knife is too dull, dear Liza, too dull.

10

Then sharpen it, dear Henry, dear Henry, dear Henry,
Then sharpen it, dear Henry, dear Henry, then sharpen it.

11

With what shall I sharpen it, dear Liza, dear Liza,
With what shall I sharpen it, dear Liza, with what?

(12)

With a whetstone, dear Henry, dear Henry, dear Henry,
With a whetstone, dear Henry, dear Henry, with a whetstone.

(13)

But the whetstone's too dry, dear Liza, dear Liza,
But the whetstone's too dry, dear Liza, too dry.

(14)

Then wet it, dear Henry, dear Henry, dear Henry,
Then wet it, dear Henry, dear Henry, then wet it.

(15)

With what shall I wet it, dear Liza, dear Liza,
With what shall I wet it, dear Liza, with what?

(16)

With water, dear Henry, dear Henry, dear Henry,
With water, dear Henry, dear Henry, with water.

(17)

How shall I get it, dear Liza, dear Liza,
How shall I get it, dear Liza, how shall I?

18

In a bucket, dear Henry, dear Henry, dear Henry,
In a bucket, dear Henry, dear Henry, in a bucket.

19

But there's a hole in the buck-et, dear Li-za, dear Li-za,
There's a hole in the buck-et, dear Li-za, there's a hole.

The Flying Trapeze

Lyrics by George Leybourne

You may be stuck in the backseat of a car right now, but you'll soon arrive at your destination and be able to walk and run around. For now, you can sing this classic circus song and imagine that you're the one who's free to fly though the air with the greatest of ease.

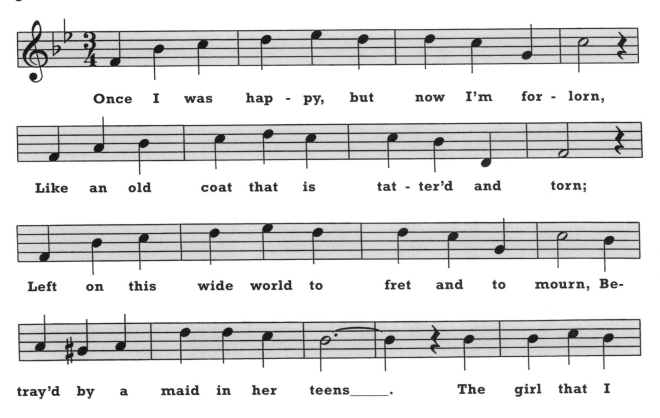

Once I was hap - py, but now I'm for - lorn,

Like an old coat that is tat - ter'd and torn;

Left on this wide world to fret and to mourn, Be-

tray'd by a maid in her teens____. The girl that I

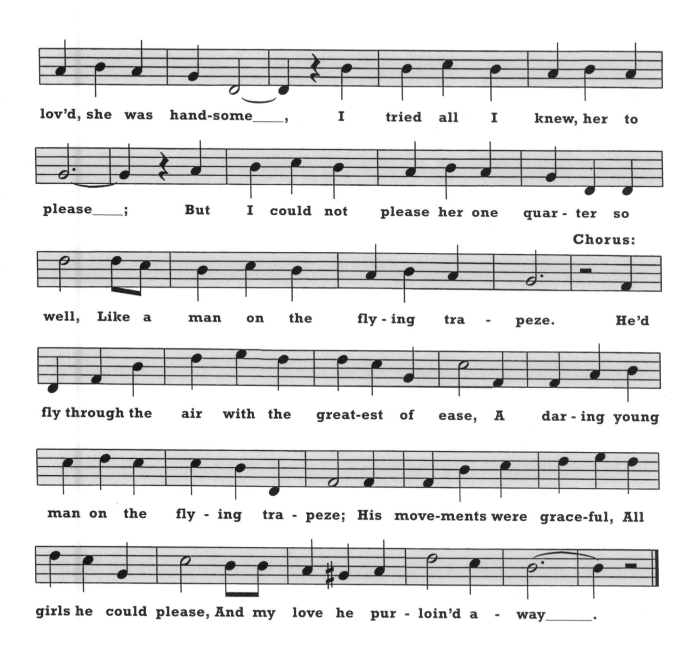

lov'd, she was hand-some___, I tried all I knew, her to

please___; But I could not please her one quar - ter so

Chorus:

well, Like a man on the fly - ing tra - peze. He'd

fly through the air with the great-est of ease, A dar - ing young

man on the fly - ing tra - peze; His move-ments were grace-ful, All

girls he could please, And my love he pur - loin'd a - way_____.

2

This young man by name was Signor Bonaslang—
Tall, big, and handsome; as well made as Chang.
Where'er he appeared, the hall loudly rang
With ovation from all people there.
He'd smile from the bar on the people below,
And one night he smiled on my love.
She winked back at him and she shouted, "Bravo!"
As he hung by his nose up above.

Chorus

3

One night I, as usual, went to her home,
Found there her father and mother alone.
I asked for my love, and soon they made known,
To my horror, that she'd run away.
She'd packed up her box and eloped in the night
With him, with the greatest of ease—
From two stories high, he had lowered her down
To the ground on his flying trapeze.

Chorus

for last verse:

She floats through the air

With the greatest of ease.

You'd think her a man on the flying trapeze.

She does all the work

While he takes his ease

And that's what became of my love.

Turkey in the Straw

Traditional American minstrel song

Grab your fiddle and stomp your feet as you sing this traditional American minstrel song that is guaranteed to turn a boring car trip into a lively hoedown!

As___ I was a-goin'_ on___ down___ the road, With a

tired__ team__ and a hea-vy___ load, I___ cracked my_ whip__ and the

lead-er sprung; I___ says "day-day"__ to the wa-gon tongue.

Chorus:

Tur-key in the straw, straw, straw, straw, Tur-key in the hay,

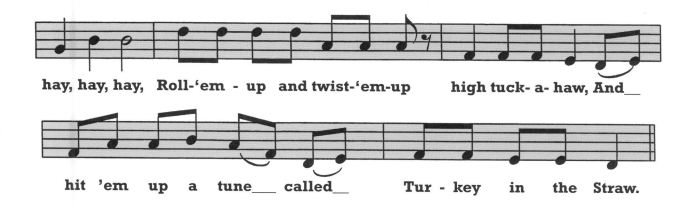

hay, hay, hay, Roll-'em - up and twist-'em-up high tuck- a- haw, And__

hit 'em up a tune___ called___ Tur - key in the Straw.

2

Went out to milk but I didn't know how,

So I milked the goat instead of the cow.

A monkey sittin' on a bale of straw

A-winkin' at his mother-in-law.

Chorus

3

I came to the river and I couldn't get across

So I paid five dollars for an old blind hoss.

Well, he wouldn't go ahead and he wouldn't stand still

So he went up and down like an old saw mill.

Chorus

4

Did you ever go fishin' on a warm summer day

When all the fish were swimmin' in the bay?

With their hands in their pockets and their pockets in their pants

Did you ever see a fishie do the Hootchy-Kootchy Dance?

Chorus

Frère Jacques

Traditional French song

Try singing this traditional French song as a two, three, or four part round.

A
Frè - re Jac - ques? Frè - re Jac - ques?

B   C
Dor - mez-vous? Dor - mez-vous? Son - nez les ma -

tin - es, Son - nez les ma - tin - es.

D
Din, din, don! Din, din, don!

ENGLISH VERSION:

Are you sleeping? Are you sleeping?

Brother John? Brother John?

Morning bells are ringing. Morning bells are ringing

Ding, dong, ding! Ding, dong, ding!

The Barnyard Song

Traditional American folk song

Make up your own verses to this American folk song by choosing more animal noises to imitate!

I had a cat and the cat pleased me,

Fed my cat un - der yon - der tree;

1
Cat went "Fid - dle - i - fee, fid - dle - i - fee."

2-4
Dog went "Bow_____ wow_____."

Cat went "Fid - dle - i - fee, fid - dle - i - fee."

2

I had a dog and the dog pleased me.

Fed my dog under yonder tree.

Dog went, "Bow wow,"

Cat went, "Fid-dle-i-fee, fiddle-i-fee."

3

I had a hen and the hen pleased me.

Fed my hen under yonder tree.

Hen went, "Ka, ka,"

Dog went, "Bow wow,"

Cat went, "Fid-dle-i-fee, fiddle-i-fee."

I had a cow and the cow pleased me.

Fed my cow under yonder tree.

Cow went, "Moo, moo,"

Hen went, "Ka, ka,"

Dog went, "Bow wow,"

Cat went, "Fid-dle-i-fee, fiddle-i-fee."

On Top of Old Smoky

Traditional

Traveling through the mountains? Sing this folk song from the Appalachians, or substitute the sillier "On Top of Spaghetti" lyrics written by Tom Glazer instead.

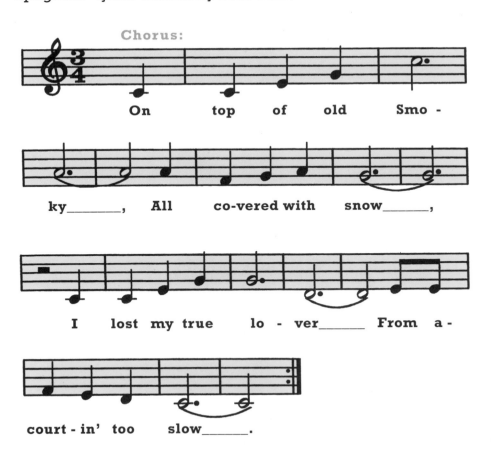

Chorus:

On top of old Smo-ky_____, All co-vered with snow_____, I lost my true lo-ver_____ From a-court-in' too slow_____.

2

On top of old Smoky
I went for to weep,
For a false-hearted lover
Is worse than a thief.

3

For a thief, he will rob you
Of all that you have,
But a false-hearted lover
Will send you to your grave.

4

He'll hug you and kiss you
And tell you more lies
Than the ties of the railroad
Or the stars in the skies.

Mama Don't Allow

Traditional

Do you get tired of people telling you not to do things? Here's a great song that's all about doing exactly what Mama says you can't do—you might even decide to sneak in a few of your own lyrics about things your mom won't allow!

Ma - ma don't al - low no mu - sic play - in' 'round here, I say that Ma - ma don't al - low no mu - sic play - in' 'round here_____. Well we don't care what Ma - ma don't al - low. Gon - na play that mu - sic a - ny - how__, Ma - ma don't al - low no mu - sic play - in' 'round here_____.

2

Mama don't allow no guitar playin' 'round here,

I say that Mama don't allow no guitar playin' 'round here.

Well we don't care what Mama don't allow.

Gonna play that guitar anyhow,

Mama don't allow no guitar playin' 'round here.

3

Mama don't allow no banjo playin' 'round here,

I say that Mama don't allow no banjo playin' 'round here.

Well we don't care what Mama don't allow.

Gonna play that banjo anyhow,

Mama don't allow no banjo playin' 'round here.

4

Mama don't allow no piano playin' 'round here,

I say that Mama don't allow no piano playin' 'round here.

Well we don't care what Mama don't allow.

Gonna play that piano anyhow,

Mama don't allow no piano playin' 'round here.

5

Mama don't allow no foot stompin' 'round here,

I say Mama don't allow no foot stompin' 'round here.

Well we don't care what Mama don't allow.

Gonna stomp my feet off anyhow,

Mama don't allow no foot stompin' 'round here.

Waltzing Matilda

Lyrics by Andrew Barton Paterson

This Australian favorite tells the story of a wanderer who stops to rest and catches a sheep. The sheep's owner and police officers soon come looking for it, and the swagman jumps into the river rather than be caught.

Once a jol - ly swag - man camped by a bil - la-bong

Un - der the shade of a coo - li - bah tree, And he

sang as he watched and wai - ted while his bil - ly boiled,

"Who'll come a-wal-tzing Ma - til - da with me? Wal - tzing Ma -

til - da, wal - tzing Ma - til - da, Who'll come a -

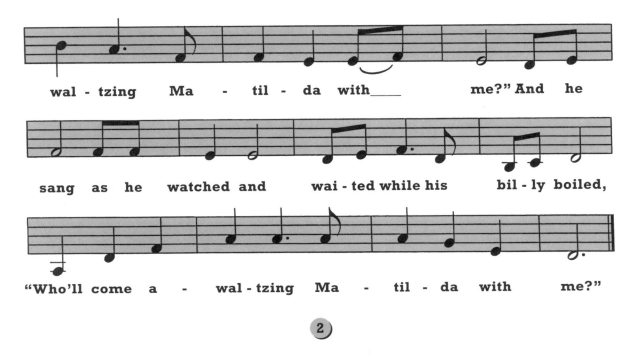

wal - tzing   Ma   -   til - da with____   me?" And   he

sang   as   he   watched and   wai - ted while his   bil - ly boiled,

"Who'll come   a   -   wal - tzing   Ma   -   til - da   with   me?"

Down came a jumbuck to drink at the waterhole.
Up jumped the swagman and grabbed him with glee,
And he sang as he stowed him away in his tucker bag,
"You'll come a-waltzing Matilda with me.
Waltzing Matilda, waltzing Matilda,
You'll come a-waltzing Matilda with me."
And he sang as he tucked that jumbuck in his tucker bag,
"You'll come a-waltzing Matilda with me."

3

Down came the stockman, riding on his thoroughbred;
Down came the troopers, one, two, three;
"Where's that jumbuck you've got in your tucker bag?

You'll come a-waltzing Matilda with me,"
Waltzing Matilda, waltzing Matilda,
You'll come a-waltzing Matilda with me.
"Where's that jumbuck you've got in your tucker bag?
You'll come a-waltzing Matilda with me."

But the swagman he up and jumped into the waterhole.
Drowning himself by the coolibah tree.
And his ghost may be heard as it sings in the billabong:
"Who'll come a-waltzing Matilda with me."
Waltzing Matilda, waltzing Matilda,
Who'll come a-waltzing Matilda with me.
And his ghost may be heard as it sings in the billabong:
"Who'll come a-waltzing Matilda with me."

The Noble Duke of York

Traditional English song

When you've reached your destination, or a rest stop along the road, stretch your legs by standing up, down, or halfway up as you hear those words in this song. For a real workout, repeat the song, singing and moving faster each time!

Oh, the no - ble Duke of York, He had ten thou - sand men; He marched them up to the top of the hill And he marched them down a - gain.

Now when they were up, they were up;

And when they were down, they were down;

And when they were only halfway up,

They were neither up nor down.

The Crawdad Song

Traditional

Wouldn't you rather be sitting by the water, looking for crayfish? Sing this lively song from the South to escape your backseat blues and imagine you're at the crawdad hole.

You get a line and I'll get a pole___, Hon-ey_____.

You get a line and I'll get a pole___, Babe_____.

You get a line and I'll get a pole, And we'll go fish-ing in the

craw-dad hole__, Hon-ey___, sug-ar ba-by mine_____.

2)

Whatcha' gonna do when the lake
runs dry, Honey?

Whatcha' gonne do when the lake runs dry, Babe?

Whatcha' gonna do when the lake runs dry?

Gonna sit on the bank and watch the crawdads die,
Honey, sugar baby mine.

3)

Yonder comes a man with a bag
on his back, Honey,

Yonder comes a man with a bag on his back, Babe,

Yonder comes a man with a bag on his back,

Carryin' all the crawdads he can pack,
Honey, sugar baby mine.

Just watch him fall down and
break his sack, Honey,

Just watch him fall down and break his sack, Babe,

Just watch him fall down and break his sack—

Wow! Look at all them crawdads crawling out,
Honey, sugar baby mine.

John Brown's Body

Traditional Civil War song

Most people think this Civil War marching song was written in honor of John Brown, the leader of the Harper's Ferry Raid, but it may have actually originated as a way to tease a Union soldier who shared his name with the famous abolitionist.

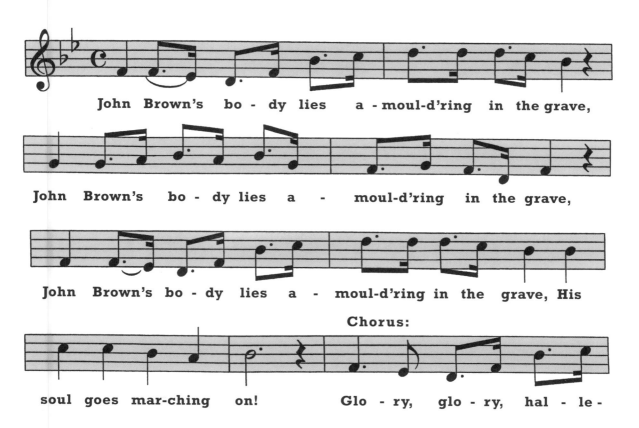

John Brown's bo - dy lies a - moul-d'ring in the grave,

John Brown's bo - dy lies a - moul-d'ring in the grave,

John Brown's bo - dy lies a - moul-d'ring in the grave, His

Chorus:

soul goes mar-ching on! Glo - ry, glo - ry, hal - le -

lu - jah! Glo - ry, glo - ry, hal - le - lu - jah!

Glo - ry, glo - ry, hal - le - lu - jah! His soul goes mar-ching on!

He's gone to be a soldier in the Army of the Lord,
He's gone to be a soldier in the Army of the Lord,
He's gone to be a soldier in the Army of the Lord,
His soul goes marching on!

Chorus

John Brown's knapsack is strapped upon his back,
John Brown's knapsack is strapped upon his back,
John Brown's knapsack is strapped upon his back,
His soul goes marching on!

Chorus

4

John Brown died that the slaves might be free,
John Brown died that the slaves might be free,

John Brown died that the slaves might be free,
His soul goes marching on!

Chorus

The stars above in Heaven now are looking kindly down,
The stars above in Heaven now are looking kindly down,
The stars above in Heaven now are looking kindly down,
His soul goes marching on!

Chorus

Alouette

Traditional French Canadian song

Here's another song with lots of verses that will make the miles speed by! It's a lively tune that mentions all the body parts of the alouette, a bird.

A - lou - et - te, gen - tille a - lou - et - te,

A - lou - et - te, je te plu - me - rai.

Je te plu - me-rai la tête, Je te plu-me - rai la tête.

Et la tête, et la tête. A - lou-ette, a - lou-ette. Ah!

2

Alouette, gentille alouette

Alouette, je te plumerai

Je te plumerai le bec

Je te plumerai le bec

Et le bec, et le bec.

Et la tête, et la tête.

Alouette, alouette.

Ah!

3

Alouette, gentille alouette

Alouette, je te plumerai

Je te plumerai les yeux

Je te plumerai les yeux

Et les yeux, et les yeux.

Et le bec, et le bec.

Et la tête, et la tête.

Alouette, alouette.

Ah!

4

Alouette, gentille alouette

Alouette, je te plumerai

Je te plumerai le cou

Je te plumerai le cou

Et le cou, et le cou.

Et les yeux, et les yeux.

Et le bec, et le bec.

Et la tête, et la tête.

Alouette, alouette.

Ah!

5

Alouette, gentille alouette

Alouette, je te plumerai

Je te plumerai le dos

Je te plumerai le dos

Et le dos, et le dos.

Et le cou, et le cou.

Et les yeux, et les yeux.

Et le bec, et le bec.

Et la tête, et la tête.

Alouette, alouette.

Ah!

6

Alouette, gentille alouette

Alouette, je te plumerai

Je te plumerai les ailes

Je te plumerai les ailes

Et les ailes, et les ailes.

Et le dos, et le dos.

Et le cou, et le cou.

Et les yeux, et les yeux.

Et le bec, et le bec.

Et la tête, et la tête.

Alouette, alouette.

Ah!

7

Alouette, gentille alouette

Alouette, je te plumerai

Je te plumerai le queue

Je te plumerai le queue

Et le queue, et le queue.

Et les ailes, et les ailes.

Et le dos, et le dos.

Et le cou, et le cou.

Et les yeux, et les yeux.

Et le bec, et le bec.

Et la tête, et la tête.

Alouette, alouette.

Ah!

8

Alouette, gentille alouette

Alouette, je te plumerai

Je te plumerai les jambes

Je te plumerai les jambes

Et les jambes, et les jambes.

Et le queue, et le queue.

Et les ailes, et les ailes.

Et le dos, et le dos.

Et le cou, et le cou.

Et les yeux, et les yeux.

Et le bec, et le bec.

Et la tête, et la tête.

Alouette, alouette.

Ah!

Alouette, gentille alouette

Alouette, je te plumerai

Je te plumerai les pattes

Je te plumerai les pattes

Et les pattes, et les pattes.

Et les jambes, et les jambes.

Et le queue, et le queue.

Et les ailes, et les ailes.

Et le dos, et le dos.

Et le cou, et le cou.

Et les yeux, et les yeux.

Et le bec, et le bec.

Et la tête, et la tête.

Alouette, alouette.

Ah!

My Bonnie Lies Over the Ocean

Traditional Scottish song

When you're taking a break from the car, this is another song that will help you stretch out your legs. Every time you sing a word that begins with the letter b, stand up or sit down—whichever you're not already doing. See how fast you can sing and move!

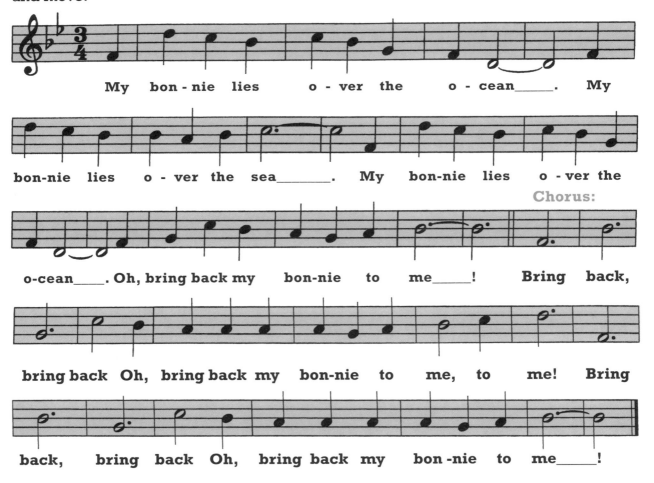

My bon-nie lies o - ver the o - cean____. My bon-nie lies o - ver the sea____. My bon-nie lies o - ver the o-cean____. Oh, bring back my bon-nie to me____! Bring back, bring back Oh, bring back my bon-nie to me, to me! Bring back, bring back Oh, bring back my bon-nie to me____!

Oh, blow ye winds over the ocean

Oh, blow ye winds over the sea

Oh, blow ye winds over the ocean

And bring back my bonnie to me.

Chorus

Last night when in bed I lay dreaming

Last night when the moon was on high

Last night when in bed I lay sleeping

I thought I heard dear bonnie cry.

Chorus

My bonnie was sleeping so soundly

My bonnie was sleeping so tight

My bonnie was sleeping so soundly

In his little crib painted white.

Chorus

The winds, they blew over the ocean

The winds, they blew over the sea

The winds, they blew over the ocean

And brought back my bonnie′ to me.

Chorus

The Animal Fair

Traditional American minstrel song

Imagine yourself at the circus as you sing this traditional American minstrel tune. Can you make up hand motions to go with these lyrics?

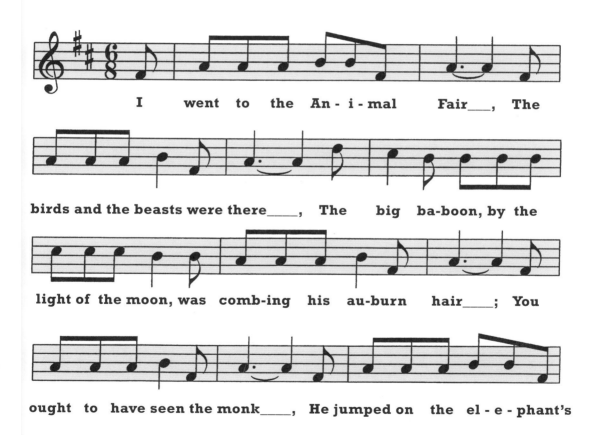

I went to the An - i - mal Fair___, The

birds and the beasts were there___, The big ba-boon, by the

light of the moon, was comb-ing his au-burn hair___; You

ought to have seen the monk___, He jumped on the el - e - phant's

trunk__; The el - e-phant sneezed and fell on his knees, And

what be - came of the monk____?

Daisy Bell

Lyrics by Harry Dacre

Harry Dacre's classic song "Daisy Bell" is filled with bicycle references like "Ped'ling away down the road of life." How many of them can you find?

There is a flow - er with - in my heart, Dai - sy,

Dai - sy! Plan - ted one day by a glanc - ing dart,

Plan-ted by Dai - sy Bell____! Wheth - er she loves me or

loves me not, Some-times it's hard to tell____. Yet I am

long - ing to share the lot of beau - ti - ful Dai - sy

Bell____! Dai - sy, Dai - sy, Give me your an - swer,

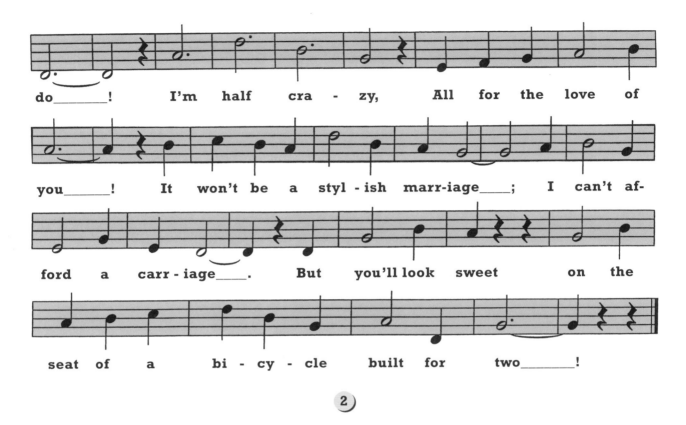

do____! I'm half cra - zy, All for the love of

you____! It won't be a styl - ish marr-iage____; I can't af-

ford a carr - iage____. But you'll look sweet on the

seat of a bi - cy - cle built for two____!

2)

We will go tandem as man and wife,
Daisy, Daisy!
Ped'ling away down the road of life,
Me and my Daisy Bell!
When the road's dark we can despise
Policeman and lamps as well;
There are bright lights in the dazzling eyes
Of beautiful Daisy Bell!

Chorus

I will stand by you in wheel or woe,

Daisy, Daisy!

You'll be the belle which I'll ring, you know!

Sweet little Daisy Bell!

You'll take the lead in each trip we take,

Then if I don't do well;

I will permit you to use the brake,

My beautiful Daisy Bell!

Chorus

What Did Delaware?

Traditional

This traditional riddle song about state names is perfect for long road trips—especially if you're driving through one of these states. Try coming up with your own riddles using state names that sound like other words!

Oh, what did Del - a - ware, boys, Oh, what did Del - a - ware? Oh,

what did Del - a - ware, boys, Oh, what did Del - a - ware? She

wore her New Jer-sey, boys, She wore her New Jer - sey. I

tell you now as a per - son - al friend, She wore her New Jer - sey.

2

Oh, what did I-o-way, boys,
Oh, what did I-o-way?
Oh, what did I-o-way, boys,
Oh, what did I-o-way?
She weighed a Wash-ing-ton, boys,
She weighed a Wash-ing-ton.
I tell you now as a personal friend,
She weighed a Wash-ing-ton.

3

Oh, what did Ten-nes-see, boys,
Oh what did Ten-nes-see?
Oh, what did Ten-nes-see boys
Oh what did Ten-nes-see?
She saw what Ar-kan-sas, boys,
She saw what Ar-kan-sas.
I tell you now as a personal friend,
She saw what Ar-kan-sas.

4

Oh, what did Ida-hoe, boys,
Oh, what did Ida-hoe?
Oh, what did Ida-hoe, boys,
Oh, what did Ida-hoe?
She hoed her Mary-land, boys,
She hoed her Mary-land.
I tell you now as a personal friend,
She hoed her Mary-land.

5

Oh, what did Massa-chew, boys,
Oh, what did Massa-chew?
Oh, what did Massa-chew, boys,
Oh, what did Massa-chew?
She chewed her Connecti-cud, boys.
She chewed her Connecti-cud.
I tell you now as a personal friend,
She chewed her Connecti-cud.

Oh, how did Flori-die, boys,

Oh, how did Flori-die?

Oh, how did Flori-die, boys,

Oh, how did Flori-die?

She died in Missouri, boys.

She died in Missouri.

I tell you now as a personal friend,

She died in Missouri.

The John B. Sails

(The Sloop John B.)

Traditional Caribbean song

Are you on the way to a tropical vacation? Do you wish you were? Singing this traditional Caribbean song will make you feel like you're sitting in the islands instead of in the car.

Oh, we came on the sloop *John B.*, My grand - fa - ther and me. 'Round Nas - sau Town____ we____ did roam. Drink-ing all night, We got in____ - to a fight. I feel so broke___ up_____, I want___ to go home.

Chorus: So hoist up the *John B.* sails.

See how the main sail sets. Send for the Cap-tain a-shore. Let_____ me go home! Let_____ me go home, Let_____ me go home. I feel so broke_ up_____, I want___ to go home.

2

The first mate, he got drunk,
Broke up somebody's trunk.
Constable came aboard and took him away.
Sergeant John Stone, please leave me alone.
I feel so broke up, I want to go home.

Chorus

3

The poor cook, he got fits,
Threw 'way all of the grits,
Then he took and ate up all of my corn.
Let me go home, I want to go home.
This is the worst trip since I've been born.

Chorus

Gee, But I Want to Go Home

Traditional U.S. Army song

This army marching song is the perfect way to give your parents the hint that you're tired of being in the car—especially if you change the chorus to "I don't want no more of backseat life, gee but I want to go home." And, it's another good one for making up your own verses!

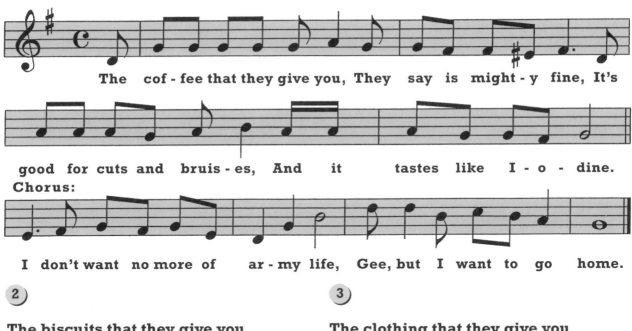

The cof - fee that they give you, They say is might - y fine, It's good for cuts and bruis - es, And it tastes like I - o - dine.

Chorus:

I don't want no more of ar - my life, Gee, but I want to go home.

2

The biscuits that they give you
They say are mighty fine;
One rolled off a table
And it squashed a pal of mine.

Chorus

3

The clothing that they give you
They say are mighty fine;
But me and my buddy
Can both fit into mine.

Chorus

4

The chickens that they give you
They say are mighty fine;
One jumped off the table
And it started marking time.

Chorus

5

The details that they give us
They say are mighty fine
The garbage that we pick up
They feed us all the time.

Chorus

6

The women in the service club
They say are mighty fine,
But most are over ninety
And the rest are under nine.

Chorus

Bon Voyage!